FATE IN YOUR HANDS

A MODERN MYTH
SHORT STORY

ALEXANDRIA BLAELOCK

BlueMere Books
MELBOURNE, AUSTRALIA

For permission requests, please contact
enquiries@bluemerebooks.com.

Ordering Information:
Discounts are available on quantity purchases. For details, contact orders@bluemerebooks.com.

Fate in Your Hands/Alexandria Blaelock
paperback ISBN: 978-1-925749-18-2
digital ISBN: 978-1-925749-19-9

Book Layout © BookDesignTemplates.com

BlueMere Books
www.bluemerebooks.com

FATE IN YOUR HANDS

Erik looked out at a seemingly endless vista of red desert, broken here and there by tussocks of spinifex.

Way off in the distance, through the shimmering heat haze, stood the odd stumpy tree.

It was hotter than it had any right to be; beating down from the sun high overhead and radiating up from the ground.

The hot air tasted like dry sand and seemed to pull all the moisture from his lungs.

Sighing, he turned to look the dilapidated weatherboard building under a sign reading "Last bookshop 1000 km."

He could tell it had been a handsome and proud home in its young glory days, but now it leant drunkenly on rotten stumps, held together by termite nests.

That it stood at all was a miracle, but that the wide veranda supported the weight of a long slatted wooden seat and the three women looking curiously at him was a wonder.

The youngest, in scarlet shorts and tank top, sat cross-legged on the left. She was in her early twenties, and her long strawberry blond hair was caught up in a messy bun on the top of her head.

She held a book in her lap, with a finger tucked in the spine to mark her place.

The woman in the middle was maybe 40. She looked tired, and her long dark hair hung loosely around her shoulders. Her black semi-fitted dress must have been stifling in the heat.

She was leaning forward, resting her chin on her folded hands on a walking stick.

On the right was a stunning woman with short white hair that seemed to dance in the rising heat. She might have been 22, 45, or maybe even 100. She sat upright yet relaxed, one leg crossed over the other. Amazingly, her loose white pants and button-down shirt were untainted by the red dust that piled up around the base of the walls.

She was idly trimming her fingernails with a small pair of scissors.

They looked at each other for a long moment before Erik shook himself and walked towards the building.

The woman in red unfolded herself from the seat and stood to meet him. That her skin could be so white in the outback was an incredible feat.

"Diana from the Palace Hotel sent me," he said. His English was good, but his Scandinavian accent fell heavily into the still air.

The young woman smiled and turned to open the door for him.

"All the books are mixed together - new and second hand in all the languages we have."

She pointed to the right, "fiction is over there," and then to the left, "non-fiction there.

"All our available stock is out, so please don't ask if we have anything else.

"Take your time, we'll be here out the front if you find something you like."

Then she turned away, leaving him in the open doorway.

He leaned forward slightly, expecting a small room with an even smaller stack of books, but instead there was an enormous room of modern shelving crammed with books.

And even more books stacked on the floor between the shelves.

Books so far as the eye could see, it was almost as if every book ever printed had been stuffed into the room.

He leaned back out to look across the width of the building before leaning back in to compare. The room was definitely bigger inside than the building.

Leaning back out, he looked at the women, who were looking at him quizzically.

The one in white made an impatient gesture towards the interior.

He smiled tentatively and nodded at them before taking a deep breath and stepping across the threshold.

Immediately he turned around, and was reassured by the continuing existence of the open door, and the view of the desert.

A flock of black cockatoos flew past screeching.

While it all seemed normal, he wanted to put his hand out the door, just to make sure it was really was a doorway and that it really was there.

Taking another deep breath, this time of book scented air, he turned towards the fiction.

His working holiday visa had almost expired, and it was time to head home to fulfil his mandatory Military Service quotient.

He'd been monitoring the political situation, and tensions had been escalating while he was away. He'd waited so long that he was just about out of time to enlist.

Perhaps if he'd joined up straight out of school, he'd have been safe, but it seemed almost certain he'd see active service on his return.

He looked at the long rows of shelves.

What he needed was something to take his mind off the fear. Something like an epic hero saga. Or a man who snatched success from the jaws of defeat.

A man who overcame his fate.

As he browsed the stacks, he could hear the faint, yet oddly comforting sound of the women's voices from the verandah.

It was kind of like being in his room as a child, hearing his mother and aunts in the kitchen, gossipping about the village as they preserved fresh produce for the winter.

He smiled slightly remembering a time he'd sat on the stairs eavesdropping. And without really thinking, he found himself listening to the women outside.

"What do you think?"

"I think he needs our help Claudia, but he has to ask for it."

"Well that's a bit harsh don't you think Agatha?"

"No such thing as a free lunch Laura."

"But Agatha—"

"Enough, we're not fairies here to grant wishes."

"Agatha, no one is saying anything about wishes."

"For heaven's sake Claudia, we can't just go around meddling in the lives of mortals. We're not gods."

"I didn't mean it like that."

"Well, what did you mean then?'

"Well, um, just that there's asking and there's asking."

"Honestly, you're slow as a wet week Claudia."

"Please Agatha. What about *earning* a favourable indulgence?"

"That's really not helping Laura."

"No really, why not?"

"Or couldn't he buy a favour with a gift?"

"Agatha, for once in your life, will you just think about it?"

"Shh. He's listening."

Silence immediately fell, as if someone had hit a cosmic mute button.

Not that he should have been eavesdropping, but it seemed everywhere he went in this country, people stopped talking when he walked into the room.

Now he was starting to think it might be him and not something that all people who live in remote towns do when strangers walk in.

What help did they expect him to ask for?

Choosing a book?

At which point, it seemed a suitably thick book jiggled on the shelf to attract his attention.

It was a dusty old hardback, the knife cut edges of its slightly textured pages were yellowed, and dog earned.

He opened the cover, and the aroma of cigar smoke, cologne and adventure rose from its pages. The vivid frontispiece of a Viking longship riding stormy seas was strangely compelling.

He flicked through the pages at random and found himself pulled into a mythic retelling of the saga of Erik the Red. He gently closed the cover and weighed the book in his hand.

Its size and weight fit comfortably into his palm, in fact, the book seemed to nestle into his hand like a lost puppy.

It seemed the perfect book had found him.

Turning to retrace his steps, he realised he'd lost sight of the door and wasn't entirely sure where it was.

Not that it isn't always possible to get lost in a good bookshop.

But given this one seemed larger than the building that housed it, it felt a more disastrous situation than one might usually suppose.

Erik giggled nervously, should he have set a string line for guidance when he struck out from the main corridor?

Clutching *Erik the Red* like a talisman and trying to swallow his panic, he reasoned that if he could hear the women talking, they couldn't be that far away.

If fiction was on the right, all he had to do was follow the path to the left, no matter how far it went, and it would lead him back to the door.

Straightening his pack on his shoulders, he clutched the book to his chest and started walking.

After a time, Erik wondered if it really was as simple as keeping to the left.

He didn't feel any closer to the door than before. The shelves were starting to look the same; lurid splashes of red and blue-toned covers with seemingly hallucinogenic gilt embossed collections of letters and symbols on the spines.

He saw a flash of red heading to the right and thinking it was the girl, chased after her.

Heart pounding, teetering on the cusp of turning the corner, he felt doubt creeping in.

Should he trust himself, or follow the girl he'd just met?

Was she trying to help him?

Was it even her, or just his imagination?

He closed his eyes, took a deep breath and held it until he could hear his blood pumping and then slowly let it out.

Choosing to believe in himself, he continued his path to the left.

He started to feel as though the shelves were closing in on him, and he couldn't catch his breath.

The back of his neck started prickling as though someone was creeping up on him.

He spun around, heart pounding wildly in his chest, but there was no one there.

The book was a solid and reassuring presence in his arms.

If Erik the Red could trust himself and take a boat into the unknown, so could he.

Mind you, Erik hadn't gone alone, he'd taken a crew to help. Each crew member had their own function, and together they'd travelled beyond the known universe and for the most part, come safely back.

Perhaps that had been what the women had been talking about. If you need help, you have to ask for it.

"Um, excuse me," he called.

The woman in black immediately stepped out from the shelves in front of him, "yes?"

Erik squeaked and stepped back.

The woman smiled faintly.

He coughed, trying to give the impression he was just clearing his throat.

"I'm sorry, you startled me. I've found a book, but I need help getting to the checkout."

"This way please," she said, disappearing around the shelving unit on his left.

He followed and found her leaning on her stick, waiting for him in a wide-open space between the shelves.

Convinced the gap he'd passed through wouldn't be there if he turned around, he focused on the startlingly ordinary country town shop in front of him.

To one side, a fridge full of cold drinks and chocolate bars hummed gently.

It was nestled between a display unit of assorted dried packaged snacks and a bent up revolving wire rack of postcards, souvenir magnets, keyrings and spoons.

On the other, an old manual cash register sat on one end of a wooden counter next to a stack of tissue paper held down by a rock.

A wall-mounted rotary fan ruffled the paper as it blew from side to side across the room.

It was all reassuringly ordinary.

And that was sort of unsettling.

Given the bigger on the inside room and the never-ending book stacks, paying and leaving wasn't going to be as easy as it looked.

He walked to the counter with the woman and passed her the book.

She weighed it in her hand; "nice choice. Did you know this is the only book he wrote?"

Erik shook his head.

"The author died shortly after it was published."

"Really? How did he die?"

"Mustard Gas poisoning, in the trenches during the First World War. It's an ugly way to die."

Erik shuddered. "I wish I didn't know that. I'm on my way home to complete my Military Service."

"Not to worry, they don't use gas these days."

He attempted a smile, "no, I suppose not. But there are still plenty of ugly ways to die in a war zone."

She took the rock off the paper and started wrapping the book. "Yes that's true. Though people die without going to war too you know."

"I guess so. I just wish the political situation at home was more stable."

She smiled sadly, "yet even knowing the risk, you're on your way home to fulfil your duty."

He smiled back, "if it's my fate to die during my service, then there's not much use fighting it is there?"

"Maybe not, but you'd be surprised just how many people do fight against their fates.

"I think it's courageous to do what you know you must, even when you're afraid of the outcome."

Erik snorted, "is it courage, or is it social pressure?"

She laughed, "I'll concede that social pressure does make a difference, but you still have to choose. Safeguarding the fates of others can never be the worst possible decision."

"And having chosen, I can move forward. There's no more reason to stand still, worrying about what's the right thing to do."

"Just so."

"Imagine that! A trip to the outback to talk Vikings and debate Kierkegaard."

She laughed again and having finished wrapping the book, sealed it with a round sticker.

"It's a bookshop in the middle of the desert, where else are you going to talk about the things that scare you?"

She put the book in a thick paper bag, pulled out the straw handles and offered it to him.

"How much do I owe you?"

"Nothing. Just take it, and get home safely."

"I can't do that, how are you supposed to make a living if you just give the stock away? You must let me pay for it."

She pursed her lips for a moment as she thought. "Well, if you're determined, perhaps you could help out with a little something that's been troubling us?"

He nodded eagerly.

"There's a big spider in the outhouse, and we'd be so grateful if you could get it out."

Erik swallowed nervously, "don't Australian spiders kill?"

She laughed again, "even if we had those kinds of spiders here, Dr Kennedy has antivenom at the surgery, and that's only an hour's drive away."

He rocked his head from side to side and reset his shoulders.

"All right, I can do this. You'd better show me where it is before I change my mind."

"I'll show you," the voice from behind him made him jump. Turning, he came face to face with the woman in white.

Her face was still and unreadable as she led him out a door he hadn't noticed before. She didn't speak as she led him down a well-worn path from the back of the building.

Silently, she pointed at the outhouse.

Its wooden walls were bleached light grey by the sun, and what remained of its door hung stiffly at an angle from one hinge. A toilet, the old-fashioned kind of lidded box with a hole in it was clearly visible.

The whole thing was festooned in spider web as though wrapped for Christmas.

He tried not to imagine a gigantic spider crawling over its roof to eat him as a snack.

"So. Are we talking about a spider as big as a saucer, or a spider as big as a mill wheel?"

The old woman snorted, "I'm pretty sure it's not even as big as the palm of my hand, but it is fast."

"Does it have a favourite spot?"

"Well, here in Australia they tend to live in small spaces, like under rocks, or between the bark and tree trunks."

"That's interesting, why do they do that?"

"Can't you feel the heat out here? During the day it's too hot to hunt, so they just hang around waiting for food to show up."

"Oookaay." He removed his backpack and dropped it to the ground. It was time to battle the monster.

He dodged back and forward a few times like a boxer and tried not to shudder in front of the old woman.

"I can do this," he said, more for his benefit than hers.

She started backing towards the house, "I'll wait for you back here."

He approached the outhouse slowly and cautiously. Still not exactly sure what he was looking for, he walked around the structure, closely inspecting the exterior walls.

Finding nothing, he had no choice but to enter it.

But for a moment, he stood still, peering inside, summoning the courage to do so.

Was it foolhardy to continue?

Could he sneak off leaving the book behind?

He discreetly glanced over his shoulder to see the old woman leaning nonchalantly, hands in her pants pockets, against the shop's back wall.

No escape that way then.

Anyway, it was just a spider, even if it was a man-eating Australian spider, how hard could it be?

Erik stood in the doorway, he licked his lips, then closed his eyes for a few seconds to give them a chance to adjust to the gloom.

He was surprised, it didn't smell unpleasantly like human excrement, more like dirt and air. It was bearable.

Opening his eyes again, he looked around the interior and saw nothing that looked like a spider.

Remembering what the old woman said about spiders living under things, he casually lifted the lid with one foot and was shocked when a spider as big as his foot launched itself from beneath it.

Momentarily paralysed by fear, he squealed as it landed on his foot. Then started screaming as it held on while he tried to hop backwards out of the toilet and flick it off at the same time.

Just as he made it out, falling over backwards, the spider flew off his foot and turning a somersault scurried off into a spinifex plant.

Erik lay screaming for an instant longer as the old woman laughed.

She trotted up the path and helped him to his feet.

"You're fine, you're fine. You've saved us from the giant monster."

He whimpered for a moment but straightened up as the other women approached.

"You've done well Erik," the old woman said, resting her hand lightly on his shoulder.

The youngest picked up his backpack and helped him into it, then the middle-aged one handed him his book bag.

"We've tested you three times," the old woman continued, "and each time you've proved yourself a man capable of facing your fear, adapting and growing."

She smiled a warm and loving smile.

"You *will* survive all that your destiny throws at you. You'll not only survive but thrive, living a long and happy life this time around.

"We're so proud of you.

"Now go back to town, and have a beer on us."

He nodded and started walking down the road, back to the town.

He was exhausted, it had been a long day, and a couple of beers in a loud, noisy bar would be just the thing before catching the bus back to the Big City in the morning.

He shuddered for a moment thinking about the spider, before enjoying the warm glow of facing and defeating his fear.

But something niggled at him, how did the old woman know what his name was?

He turned back, but as he half expected, the bookshop was gone.

Only the desert remained, crisscrossed by skittered lizard tracks.

He smiled, surviving and thriving was what it was all about then.

He'd survived this, he could survive anything.

THE END

ABOUT THE AUTHOR

Alexandria Blaelock writes stories, some of them for *Ellery Queen's Mystery Magazine* and *Pulphouse Fiction Magazine*. She's also written four self-help books applying business techniques to personal matters like getting dressed, cleaning house, and feeding your friends.

As a recovering Project Manager, she's probably too fond of sticking to plan. She lives in a forest because she enjoys birdsong, the scent of gum leaves and the sun on her face. When not telecommuting to parallel universes from her Melbourne based imagination, she watches K-dramas, talks to animals, and drinks Campari. At the same time.

Discover more at www.alexandriablaelock.com.

OTHER SHORT STORIES BY ALEXANDRIA BLAELOCK

Kiss of Death
Long Weekend in the Snow
Shining Star
Phoenix Child
Ship in a Bottle
Lady of the Looking Glass
Simone Says Hands in the Air
Life in the Security Directorate
Fate in Your Hands
Love in the Security Directorate
Alma's Grace
Payton's Run
The Guardian's Vigil
The Life and Death of Carmelita Basingstoke
Balancing the Book

BOOKS BY
ALEXANDRIA BLAELOCK

Stress Free Dinner Parties
Build Your Signature Wardrobe
Holistic Personal Finance
Ms Blaelock's Book of Minimally Viable
Housekeeping